MAE AND THE MOON

by Jami Gigot

Ripple Grove Press
Portland, OR

For Mae and Sebastien

–J.G.

First Edition 2015

Library of Congress Control Number 2014949187
ISBN 978-0-9913866-2-8

10 9 8 7 6 5 4 3 2 1
Printed in South Korea by PACOM

This book was typeset in Kiddish.
The illustrations were rendered in pencil and digital paint.
Book designed by Jami Gigot

Ripple Grove Press
Portland, OR

Visit us at www.RippleGrovePress.com

Mae loved the night sky and finding the moon.

She thought the moon was following her, because whenever she looked up, the moon was not far behind.

Mae didn't mind being followed.
She liked the moon very much.

Sometimes Mae tried to catch the moon, but the moon was far too clever to be caught.

So Mae lay down in the cool night grass and gazed up in wonder.

They often played games together.

Their favorite game was hide-and-seek.

As the nights passed, Mae noticed that the moon was changing. It was getting thinner, until one night all that was left was a silver crescent.

The next night, the moon was . . .

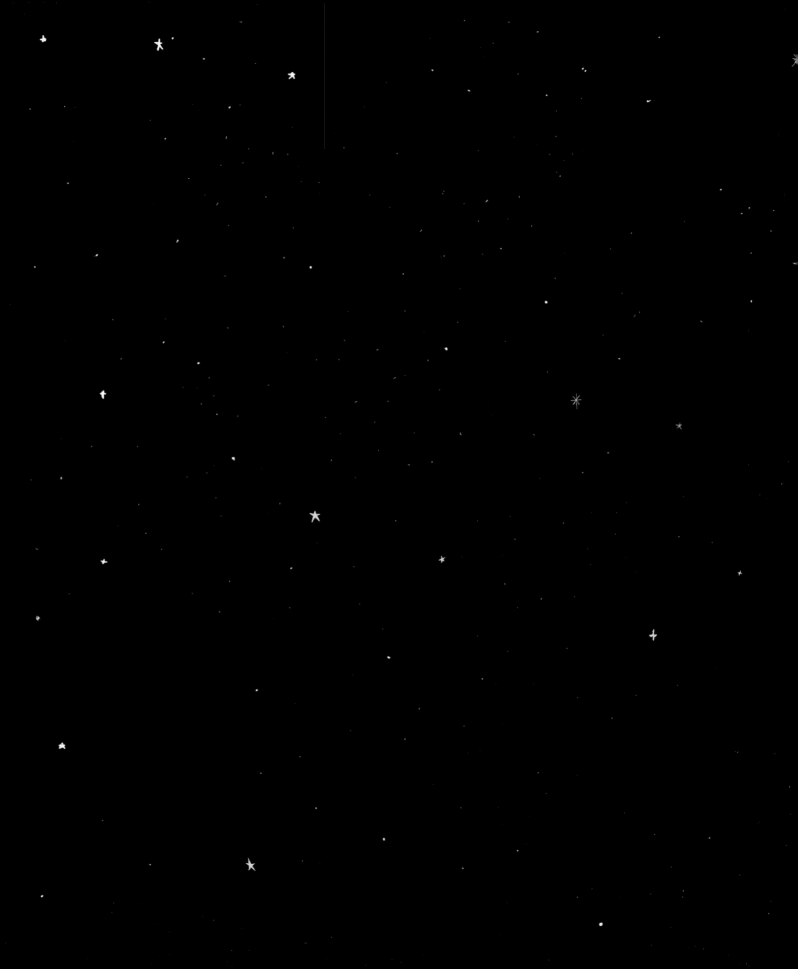

gone.

"Will the moon come back?" Mae asked.
"Even moons need to rest," said her mom.

But Mae could not rest.

GLOW STICKERS

How to Build a Rocket

That night she made a plan . . .

and the next day
she got straight to work.

"All right, Mae, time to go in," called Papa. "It's getting late."

"But, Papa, we are on our way to find the . . .

"Moon!" Mae squealed with delight. She was so busy playing, she hadn't noticed the moon was back and shining brightly.

"I missed you, moon.
I'm so happy you're back," Mae whispered with a smile.

And the moon smiled back.